Acknowledgements

Thanks to Dawn Spears the brilliant artist who created the cover artwork and my editor Debz Hobbs-Wyatt.

My wife who is so supportive and believes in me. Last my dogs Blaez and Zeeva and cats Vaskr and Rosa who watch me act out the fight scenes and must wonder what the hell has gotten into their boss. And a special thank you to Troy who was the Grandfather of Blaez in real life. He was a magnificent beast just like his grandson!

THANK YOU FOR READING!

I hope you enjoy reading this book as much as I enjoyed writing it. Reviews are so helpful to authors. I really appreciate all reviews, both positive and negative. If you want to leave one, you can do so on Amazon, through the website, or also on Twitter.

About the Author

Christopher C Tubbs is a dog-loving descendent of a long line of Dorset clay miners and has chased his family tree back to the 16th century in the Isle of Purbeck. He left school at sixteen to train as an Avionics Craftsman, has been a public speaker at conferences for most of his career and was one of the founders of a successful games company back in the 1990s. Now in his sixties, he finally writes the stories he had been dreaming about for years. Thanks to inspiration from great authors like Alexander Kent, Dewey Lambdin, Patrick O'Brian, Raymond E Feist, and Dudley Pope, he was finally able to put digit to keyboard. He lives in the Netherlands with his wife, two Dutch Shepherds, and two Norwegian Forest cats.

You can visit him on his website
www.thedorsetboy.com

The Dorset Boy, Facebook page.

Or tweet him @ChristopherCTu3

Contents

Chapter 1: A Diamond Opportunity

"That will be sixteen pounds, Mr Griffon. Would you like me to charge it to your account?" Archibald Manton, purveyor of firearms and weapons in general asked Charlemagne Griffon. Griffon was a regular customer; tall at six feet, athletically built and good looking. He looked every inch the adventurer he was reputed to be.

Charlie, as he liked to be called, picked up the boxes containing his new Remington Model 1858 .36 calibre revolvers, spare cylinders, tools and bullet moulds. "Charge it to my account please, Archibald, I will settle up at the end of the month as usual."

"Very good, sir, I am sure you will enjoy using those little beauties."

He would indeed, these 'little beauties' increased the firepower at his disposal immensely. They had only recently hit the market and were a revolution in personal weapons.

He tucked the boxes under his arm and walked down the street towards a shop that sold leather goods. He was pondering how to holster the pistols when a cloud of steam and smoke unexpectedly engulfed him making him cough. The horseless carriage that pulled up at the kerb was coal powered, a relic, as all boilers made in the last five years were gas fired. A man stepped out and approached him, "Griffon! Is that you, old chap?"

The cloud parted to reveal a gaudily-dressed man in a long scarlet coat open to reveal a heavily-embroidered waistcoat held together by gold clasps. On his head he wore a top hat decorated with a pheasant feather and pince nez glasses dangled from a gold chain around his neck.

"Felix. It could only be you in that stinker, why don't you get it updated?" Charlie said.

Felix Mountbank was an archivist, researcher and bon vivant. He was one of Charlie's oldest acquaintances.

"No time, old boy, is that a public house over there? We need to talk." The driver of the 'stinker' gave him a wave and the beast smoked and chuffed its way down the street to one of the public parking areas.

If Felix had something to say he would certainly listen, the man was a bottomless source of information. He led him to the pub and got ready to pay for a substantial lunch.

"Whitebait followed by beef, onion and oyster pie, boiled spuds, braised cabbage and mashed swede for me please," Felix said in reply to the waiter's enquiry, "and a pint of your excellent porter."

"I'll have the same, except I would prefer a glass of burgundy," Charlie said then turned to Felix.

"So, what has gotten you out of Oxford and up here to London and how did you find me?"

"Finding you was the easy part. I called at your house and that overly loyal man of yours, what's his name?"

"Etherton."

"Etherton told me you were in town picking up some new weaponry. There was only a couple of places that could be, and I hit the bullseye first shot."

"Well done, and now why?"

Felix looked around to make sure no one was in hearing. "I was researching the history of the Silk Road when I came across something that should be of utmost interest to you. It's in the Karakoram Mountains."

Charlie frowned, "That's not part of the British Empire."

"No, and that's where you come in. The mountains border China, India and Afghanistan and are disputed territory. To complicate things, the Russians are claiming Afghanistan as part of their empire even though the locals may not agree. Anyway, there is a Buddhist temple hidden away near a mountain called Malubiting. It has been lost for the last hundred years but I found an old manuscript that describes where it is."

"You want me to go there and retrieve something?"

Felix bent closer and passed him a folded paper. "Inside the temple is a statue of Buddha."

"You want me to take the statue?"

Felix huffed impatiently. "Concealed inside, under, or close to the statue is a relic, a diamond that is purported to have been created by Buddha himself from a lump of coal to show how worthless such trinkets are."

"How big is this diamond supposed to be?"

"As big as Buddha's fist, hence the name."

Charlie unfolded the paper and traced on it was a map with annotations against features and notations around the border.

"I found that in the ancient scroll. Took me hours to trace it and translate all the text."

"Why do we want this diamond?"

"Because the Russians have found out about it and that Fabergé fellow wants it to create some meaningless trinket out of it."

"Why is that a problem?"

"Because he will cut it into smaller diamonds and the relic will be lost forever!"

"Oh, I see! It's a rescue mission!"

"The British Museum will pay you handsomely."

Now it made sense, the museum had a voracious appetite when it came to acquiring other nations' treasures. Especially ones that belonged to, or were sought by, competitors of the British Empire.

Lunch completed, he finished his shopping, he had decided on shoulder holsters, and got a cab back to his home in Whitechapel. As the cab trundled along the street, rumbling over the cobbles, he found himself thinking of Samantha, his current love interest. She was not going to be happy. He had just returned from a trip to India where he had been part of an exhibition to explore the source of the River Ganges. It had been run by Professor Hamish McLagan of Edinburgh University and he had been taken partly for his ability as an explorer but more, he suspected, for his fighting ability. They had not found the source, being defeated by the sheer ferocity of the rapids they came upon as they climbed into the hills. It would have been a failure as a trip if he hadn't managed to receive a present of some rather good sapphires from a Maharaja's daughter. Something else Samantha didn't need to know about. He had been home a scant three weeks.

Samantha Quinlan was the daughter of Seamus Quinlan the head of the London Irish, one of the city's four main criminal gangs. The Irish controlled the criminal activities of most of Whitechapel and Saffron Hill, Poplar and Southwark and were headquartered in the Calmel Buildings off Orchard Street in Marylebone.

She was a dark-haired, blue-eyed firecracker of a colleen who knew her own mind, which is to say she had been spoilt rotten by her father since her mother died when she was just two years old. They had been stepping out for about two years now and she had been dropping hints about making the relationship permanent. Unfortunately for Samantha, even though he was very fond of her, marriage was the last thing on his mind.

The cab pulled up at the kerb with a squeal of brakes as the shoes pressed on the steel rims of the wheels, and the cabbie called down from his seat up front, "We're here guv, that'll be a tanner please."

Charlie opened the door, let himself out and delved into his waistcoat pocket for a sixpence. He handed up the coin and a penny tip as his man, Etherton, came out of his front door and gathered the packages from the cab.

"Thank you, kindly guv." The cabbie grinned and as soon as he heard the door close, engaged the gears and had it chuffing and trundling down the road to his next fare.

Charlie called to Etherton as he took off his coat, "Pack the mountain gear, we are off again."

Etherton turned and looked alarmed, mouth open to say something when the door to his drawing room opened, "So, you'll be after running away again will you?"

Etherton assumed a look of strict neutrality and turned back to taking the packages to the armoury. The house, quite normal from the outside, was most unusual on the inside. The cellar housed an extensive reference library and armoury. The armoury was secured behind a thick steel door with one of the new combination locks. Along two walls were a selection of weapons collected during their many trips around the world and included swords, knives, bows, crossbows, guns of all types and calibres and some exotic devices that defied classification.

There was a worktable in the centre where weapons could be maintained and a large selection of tools. There was a lay shaft running across one wall at ceiling height that powered various machine tools via belts. The shaft was powered by a small steam engine that was fed from the house's central boiler.

Etherton unpacked the pistols and put them to one side. Another package held a leather harness arrangement with two sprung holsters that would allow the Remingtons to be worn under one's jacket. The harness also had pockets for spare cylinders. He examined the guns. A lever under the barrel allowed the removal of the cylinder, allowing a pre-loaded one to be fitted quickly: a nice feature which would give the shooter a rapid-reload capability. The chambers were fired by percussion caps. He loaded all the chambers but left the percussion caps off.

Upstairs Charlie was having a much less pleasant time of it.

"You've been back three weeks after being away for four months and you are going again?"

"I didn't plan—"

"Oh, I bet you didn't! You didn't plan to stay around because you didn't want to be with me!"

"That's not—"

"Not what? Not the way you planned to tell me?"

Charlie did the only thing he could to stop the torrent, he kissed her, soundly.

"And don't you think you can—"

He kissed her again.

"You will be away for your birthday," she murmured.

"I will be back for yours."

The kissing continued.

A discreet cough from the door and Etherton announced in his South London accent, "Miss Samantha's father is approaching. I believe he intends to visit."

"How does he do that?" Samantha asked, "He was in the cellar just a minute ago."

Charlie didn't answer, what she didn't know was that he had installed a camera obscura that could be turned to provide a live view around the outside of the house. A new piece of optical engineering that he had snapped up as soon as he saw it even if it meant extensive modifications to his house.

Sure, enough there was a knock at the door and Seamus' voice boomed out,

"Charlie, is my daughter here with you?"

Etherton opened the door after giving Charlie and Samantha time to compose themselves.

"Morning, Charlie," Seamus said and turned straight to Samantha, "you are supposed to be entertaining your aunt! The damn woman is driving me crazy, with her 'you should do this' or 'your brother wouldn't do that'. I swear if I have to put up with her for much longer, she will end up in the Thames!"

Samantha rolled her eyes and said, "Sorry, Charlie, I have to go to Aunt Martha." She kissed him chastely on the cheek.

Once she left, he turned to Seamus. "I suppose you need somewhere to hide for a bit?"

"Ay, I could do at that, the damn woman is unstoppable and unbearable."

Charlie stepped to the door and cocked his head for Seamus to follow. He led him deeper into the house, down the stairs to the cellar and into the armoury. A concealed switch allowed a rack of swords and knives to swing to one side to reveal what looked at first sight to be a tunnel. Charlie turned a valve and gaslights revealed it was in fact a shooting range. Eight feet across, ten feet high and one hundred feet long with an earth wall at the far end, it was equipped with a pulley system to send targets to whatever distance down the tunnel you wanted. An extractor fan mounted in the ceiling, powered from the lay shaft, pulled the gunpowder smoke out through a shaft that connected with the chimney of the boiler.

"I got these this morning," Charlie said and showed Seamus the Remington pistols, "fancy giving them a try?"

Seamus' face broke into a grin, this is why he liked Charlie he had all the best big boys' toys.

"You first, boy."

Charlie passed him a pair of cork earplugs then took a pistol and fitted percussion caps. He picked up a second cylinder, repeated the exercise, dropped it in his waistcoat pocket, stepped to the threshold of the range and took his position. The target was set to fifty feet. He raised the gun single handed, arm straight, wrist braced and pulled the hammer back to full cock with his thumb. Manton had told him they had been sighted for seventy-five yards. A gentle steady pressure on the trigger. His first shot was high and to the right.

He cocked and fired again. This one clipped the line of the bull top right. The third, fourth and fifth were clustered in the centre.

He pulled the lever below the barrel down and removed the spent cylinder swapping it for the full one in his pocket. Once the gun was loaded and the lever returned to the secure position, he sent the target another twenty-five feet down range and fired the next five rounds.

"Not bad!" Seamus said as they examined the remains of the target, "My turn."

Seamus asked for the new target to be set directly at seventy-five feet and sent five bullets down almost as fast as he could cock the hammer. His second five followed just as quickly.

"Well he is certainly dead," Charlie laughed as the target came back on the pulley system. The target had the outline of a man with a bullseye over the heart. Seamus' had ten holes, all inside the outline with just two inside the bullseye.

"Dead is what matters, boyo," Seamus grinned. "Do you have a full cylinder?"

Charlie passed him one from the table which Seamus fitted. He stepped to the threshold and holding the gun at waist height, his elbow pressed into his side, fired all five rounds by holding in the trigger and cocking the gun with the heal of his hand in a fanning motion.

"That would be very useful in a bar fight. Why do you leave one chamber empty?"

"I'll show you."

Charlie took his gun and held it at waist height, pointing down range. The hammer at rest on a loaded chamber. He took a small hammer and gently tapped the back of the hammer. The gun fired.

"If you just jog the hammer when its resting on a live chamber these things will fire, so you leave one chamber empty for safety. Saves getting shot in an embarrassing place."

Chapter 2: The Road to Bombay

That evening, after Seamus had left, Charlie and Etherton were in the library poring over maps and the timetables for trains and ships. Charlie had traced their route on a large map.

"We can take a steam packet to Karachi then a boat up the Indus as far as we can, then it's horses for the rest of the way. We will need local guides, but they can be found when we get there."

"I will arrange tickets this afternoon," Etherton said.

"Go to Manton's and get yourself at least one revolver as well. We will be going into bandit country."

That evening Charlie was sorting out what he would be taking. They would travel light and buy locally anything they needed. The main reason being that locally-made clothes suited the local conditions better than anything they could get in London. The second reason was they wanted to use their baggage allowance for equipment.

"I have got us tickets for the Thursday packet from Southampton, it leaves at two in the afternoon so we can get the train from Waterloo in the morning and be there in time."

"What cabins have you got?"

"They only had one left, a stateroom."

"So, we are sharing?"

"Yes, I will pack earplugs against your snoring."

Charlie didn't bite, he knew that Etherton was only half joking as he did have a tendency to snore especially if he had been drinking. Sharing was nothing new, in the early days when they first started adventuring, they had to share as Charlie didn't have the money for separate rooms. Etherton had been his batman in the army and had followed him out when he had been cashiered for punching out a fellow officer for abusing his men.

An accident; a pair of steam waggons collided, causing one to shed its load – sacks of flour – blocking the road. They would miss their train if they waited for it to be cleared so abandon their cab and walked around the blockage to find another on the other side. A risky exercise as there was always a chance the gas tanks on the steam waggons could explode. They enlisted a couple of passing barrow boys to shift their luggage.

Now they were settled in their first-class carriage and Etherton was ordering tea from the steward.

"We have a new variety of tea if sir would be interested. It is China keemun tea flavoured with Bergamot also known as the Earl Grey blend."

"I have heard of it, you would drink it black I believe," Charlie said, "I will take a pot. What will you have, Etherton?"

"A pot of English breakfast and some milk for me."

Charlie grinned his 'man' would never leave his working-class roots.

Etherton insisted on serving him and shooed the steward away as soon as the tea arrived.

"I honestly thought we would miss it," Charlie said as he savoured the floral and slightly citrus tea.

"It was close, I believe they were running a little late which made the difference." He paused as he noticed a man stood in the corridor looking at them through the glass upper half of the compartment wall. He was dressed in a heavy overcoat with a fur collar, a bowler hat with goggles resting on the brim. Charlie took in his features in a single glance, he had the ability to recognise someone after only the shortest glimpse of their face and this one he would definitely remember. Angular features, a hook nose, monobrow, piercing blue eyes, scar on the left cheek.

The watcher turned and walked towards the front of the train.

"I believe we may have company for this trip."

They didn't see the man again but even so, as they disembarked at Southampton Central station, they cast a wary eye over the crowd before stepping down onto the platform. Etherton instructed a porter to take their trunks to a cab.

The port was a short ride away and had an airfield at the end. Dirigibles floated overhead; streams of steam vapour marking their course. The cab followed from below and entered the port through a large ornate wrought iron gate. The guard saluted and bowed them through. Both men checked their guns; Charlie his brace of Remington Navy revolvers, and Etherton his new seven shot .31 calibre Remington pocket version and his favourite double-barrelled pistol gripped, .75 calibre, breach loaded man stopper made by Egg of London. Charlie often joked that it wasn't a pistol but a hand cannon.

The cab jolted to a halt at dock three where the mail packet sailed from. The *King George IV*, a hybrid sail and steam schooner, sat at the dock with a swarm of stevedores loading cargo and the supplies needed for the six-week leg to Cape Town. Their luggage was taken by porters to the embarkation desk where their tickets were checked, and the trunks labelled. That would be the last time they would see them until they got to their cabin.

Ships were still using coal and the smell of smoke drifted over them on the onshore breeze from not only the *King George IV* but from the steam tugs that hovered in attendance, ready to help her get to sea.

Charlie and Etherton were met by a steward at the top of the gangplank and shown to their state room. Two bedrooms with their own bathrooms and a sitting room provided all the luxuries of home. The luggage was already stacked in the sitting room. Charlie left Etherton to deal with that and went up on deck for departure.

He found his way to the first-class observation deck in time to see the tugs start to pull the ship away from the dock. Communicating by toots on their steam whistles, the tugs eased the ship away from the dock and turned her, so she pointed towards the sea.

A movement out the corner of his eye alerted Charlie that someone else was coming out onto the deck. It was the man from the train. Charlie slowly brought his left hand up and inside his coat where it rested on the butt of a pistol.

The man, however, didn't even look at him but just watched the family and friends of the passengers who lined the rail below on the main deck shouting their goodbyes and waving from the dock. Charlie relaxed. If he was on this deck then he would be known by the stewards.

He felt the ship's engines start to push her forward and smoke billowed from the funnel. They were on their way. He turned around to look at the land for one last time and the world went black.

"Aah you are back with us," a voice came out of the darkness as he cracked his eyes open. His head hurt and he felt sick.

The world came into focus and Etherton and a man in the white uniform of the ship's crew came into view.

"What?"

"We think you slipped and hit your head. Reginald Warburton, ship's doctor," the uniform said as he helped Charlie sit up. He looked around; he was in his state room on the chaise longue.

"They found you on the observation deck," Etherton said.

"Was there anyone else there?"

"No."

"Well now you are back in the land of the conscious I will leave you to it, there are some painkillers on the table if you need them."

Once he left Charlie looked at Etherton, "The man from the train was there, and as only first-class passengers are allowed on that deck he must be known by the stewards."

"I will ask around," Etherton said. "Oh by the way, your pockets had been searched. He must have been disturbed because he left your trouser pocket lining hanging out."

"Probably looking for the map, did he take my guns?"

"No, but he did remove the percussion caps."

Charlie stood, carefully, and crossed to where his coat was thrown over a chair. The leather tailcoat was the latest fashion and had a high upright collar. It had been made for him by his tailor, Gideon Cohen, and contained several concealed pockets, one of which was in the collar. He ran his fingers along the seam until he found the opening and pulled out the map.

"Still here." He unfolded it to make sure it hadn't been replaced.

"It's probably as safe there as it is anywhere," Etherton said from the table where he was stripping Charlie's guns and meticulously checking every part.

Charlie folded the map and returned it to the collar pocket. He had memorised it and could probably reproduce it but that could lead to errors or omissions, so he was keen to keep it safe.

Nothing else happened until they got to Cape Town. They went ashore with the rest of the passengers while the ship coaled. The chance to stretch one's legs on solid ground was irresistible.

Etherton had discretely asked the stewards who else was in first class and no one matching the description of 'the man' was travelling there. He also spent some time watching the steerage class passengers and he wasn't among them either. It was a mystery.

On their return to their cabins, it was obvious to them that someone had gone through their luggage and cupboards. The room was still tidy so whoever had done it was a professional, but what he didn't know was that they always left tell tales to show if anything had been disturbed.

"Every drawer has been opened as has the wardrobe," Etherton said.

"And all the trunks have been opened. The lining in the lid of this one has been slit along the edge."

It was frustrating, Charlie knew *their stalker*, as he had come to think of him, was on the ship but so far, they had been unable to find him. It wasn't that it was a big ship, it wasn't, there were only sixty passengers. Ten in first class, mainly senior company men or army officers and their wives who would leave when they stopped in Bombay. He had met all of them over dinner and the social events that kept the passengers amused during the voyage. Etherton had met their servants. Steerage class was made up of clerks, junior officers, and fortune seekers. Mostly single men, none of whom looked remotely like the stalker.

That left the possibility that he was crew but again they didn't see him amongst the visible ones. It could be he was an engineer down in the boiler room, those poor souls hardly ever saw the light of day, or he could be a stowaway. If he was, he must have the help of someone on the crew.

The trip progressed and the ship passed between Madagascar and the African coast. Two new first-class passengers joined at Cape Town and Charlie met him and his lady companion over dinner.

"Charlie Griffon," Charlie said as they sat at the pristinely-set dinner table. His new dinner companions were well dressed, the man in a well-cut long brocade jacket, black shirt with mother of pearl buttons and deep red cravat held in place with a gold pin mounted with a large ruby. She in a scandalous blue satin, tight bodice dress that exposed her shoulders and pushed up her breasts, the skirt was ruched and stopped above her knees at the front while dipping almost to her ankles at the back. She wore calf-length, button-up high-heeled boots and stockings to complete her look. It was expensive and provocative. She had, he couldn't fail to notice, the hint of a tattoo peeking out from under the bodice on her cleavage. Her make-up was dark and aggressive, challenging even.

"Benedict Cumberland-Smythe, my companion Annabelle Darwimple," the slim elegant man with a goatee beard said.

"Delighted I'm sure, you joined at Cape Town, but you don't sound like natives."

"You are very observant," Annabelle purred, she had a deep voice and Charlie detected the edge of an accent he couldn't identify. "We are on a world tour and Cape Town was at the end of the African stage."

He wasn't sure, but the way she leaned towards him and looked at him with those ice blue eyes could be interpreted as inviting. He decided to reserve judgement. His attention was drawn back to Cumberland-Smythe,

"Have you travelled from England?"

"Yes, I joined in Southampton."

"You have business in India?"

"Just sightseeing and a bit of mountaineering."

"Ooh that's interesting, mountaineering sounds so exciting," Annabelle simpered.

That doesn't sit well on her, she is definitely not the simpering type.

"It can be, but most climbers would prefer it if it doesn't get too exciting, the point is to get to the top and back again."

"Where in India do you climb?" Cumberland-Smythe said.

After the dinner Charlie returned to his cabin and told Etherton of the new passengers.

"I doubt those are their real names and they have a hint of an accent when they say certain words. He tends to make a 'w' out of 'v' and she rolls her r's."

The next evening neither Cumberland-Smythe or Annabelle were at dinner and he found himself alone, savouring a good brandy and a cigar on the observation deck watching the stars.

"There you are, I was looking for you," Annabelle's silky voice came from just behind him.

He turned and looked at her in surprise, he hadn't heard her come onto the deck. She moved in closer until she was almost touching him. He could smell her perfume, floral with a hint of musk, definitely sexy. She was tall, probably five feet six or seven in bare feet which meant that in her four-inch heels she was almost as tall as him.

"How do you move so quietly in those heels?"

"Practice, I am a dancer."

"Really I guess that means you are really flexible." *Two can play this game.*

"Very."

She rolled the R!

Annabelle leant forward so her breasts were brushing his chest and looked up into his eyes; her lips parted.

"Wont Benedict miss you?"

"He is not well, sea sickness, confined to his bed."

He could feel her breath on his lips, it smelt very faintly of fish.

"I am bored, and I think you can amuse me."

She moved in the last inch and kissed him.

"On the observation deck?" Etherton said in amazement.

"She wasn't wearing much under her dress."

"But on the deck?"

"When did you get to be a prude?"

Etherton huffed and busied himself brushing down the jacket that had been creased in the encounter.

"She is Russian you know." Charlie leaned back in his chair with his hands behind his head.

"How do you come to that conclusion?"

"She tasted of caviar; it took me a while to identify it, but it was definitely Beluga caviar. They don't have any on this ship so they must have it in their cabin.

"Were you carrying a gun?"

"No,"

"That was lucky, wouldn't want a premature detonation."

"Ha, ha, very funny. She also rolls her R's when she gets excited."

"Do we still have the map?"

"Yes, it's in the lid of the trunk that they slit open last time they searched the cabin."

Etherton went to the trunk and checked, "Still there."

"She wants us to meet here next time."

"If she is Russian, she is probably working for the opposition."

"Oh, I am certain of that," Charlie grinned, "but she is a damn good lover."

Etherton rolled his eyes, "Just be careful what you say."

"I wasn't thinking of doing any talking."

Before he had the chance for a second dalliance, Etherton came with news, "I've seen him,"

He caught Charlie unawares, "Who?"

"Our mystery stalker."

That got Charlie's full attention, "Where?"

"Going into your girlfriend's cabin."

"You were watching it?"

"Of course, if they are the competition, I want to know everything I can about them. Unlike some people."

Charlie frowned, "We will stop at Bombay in two days, I think we need to try something to force the issue."

Etherton sighed, this could go horribly wrong, but Charlie had luck which might swing the odds their way.

That evening over dinner he pointedly ignored Cumberland-Smythe and let Annabelle know he wanted to see her by clumsily passing a note across the table when her paramour wasn't supposed to be watching. The gasps from the other people on the table as he did it told him he was.

"What is that?" Benedict asked and held out his hand. Annabelle didn't even pretend to look chagrined and handed it over. He read it aloud. "Meet me in my cabin at nine o'clock?" He stood knocking his chair over.

"You are a cad, sir!" He strode around the table to stand behind Charlie's chair, "Stand and face me!"

Charlie obliged, unfolding his six-foot frame until he stood over the shorter man. He could hear mutterings around the table of "I say!" and "Well I never!" from the ladies. The men sat back with eager anticipation on their faces, this was probably the most entertainment they'd had for weeks.

"I demand satisfaction!" Benedict followed up the demand with a slap across Charlie's face.

Charlie's eyes went flat and hard, his expression cruel, "Naturally, I will meet you at dawn tomorrow on the observation deck. What is your weapon of choice?"

Uncertainty flashed in Benedict's eyes for just a second and was swiftly replaced with cunning. "Pistols, I have a pair of duelling pistols in my luggage."

"I don't think so, we will use these."

Charlie pulled his Remingtons from their shoulder holsters to gasps and exclamations from the watching diners.

"We will stand twenty feet apart and shoot on the command from our master of ceremonies. Who, I suggest, should be the good colonel here. As a military man he will know the form and be impartial."

Benedict was cornered, only one chamber would be loaded under the scrutiny of the M.C.. Colonel Farrington would be scrupulously fair and ensure that everything was done to the letter of the law. He even took possession of the pistols to prepare them in front of the nominated seconds.

The following morning, Charlie arrived on the observation deck five minutes before the allotted time. The weather was fair, and the deck hardly rolled. Colonel Farrington and Warburton the ship's doctor were already there with his guns on a folding table.

"Can we confirm the rules?" Charlie said as he saw Cumberland-Smythe step out of the door from the first-class dining room.

"Of course. The combatants will stand on the marks I have already put on the deck. Pistols may not be cocked or brought to the ready until the command 'shoot.' The duel will be considered over when either both pistols are fired or one of the combatants is unable to proceed.

"Excellent!" Charlie grinned and sauntered over to where Etherton waited.

Annabelle arrived. If she was upset by the prospect of one of her lovers getting shot, she didn't show it. She was dressed in a black and red, racy dress, the skirt of which was cut high at the front and low at the back, exposing her legs that were encased in fishnet stockings. Etherton sniffed at the sight and left the deck.

"Gentlemen, it is time!" Farrington announced in a loud voice.

The whole of first class lined the deck, some of the steerage passengers, who had heard that there was a duel, had climbed up into the rigging and were hooting and hollering their support.

Charlie shed his coat, handing it to the nearest passenger. He was wearing his shoulder holsters.

"Choose your weapons!" Farrington commanded in a parade-ground bark.

"After you, old boy," Charlie said acknowledging the right of the challenger for first choice. Cumberland-Smythe looked at both guns suspiciously and hesitated, sure there was a trick somewhere.

"Both guns have been prepared equally," Farrington snapped.

He chose one and walked to his mark.

Charlie picked up the other and nonchalantly clipped it in the holster on the left side of his chest after checking the cylinder. He walked to his mark and made a show of waving to the crowd and blowing a kiss to Annabelle.

Against standard practice, which dictated you stood side-on, he faced his opponent square-on.

Cumberland-Smythe adopted the traditional stance, side-on, gun held low. He looked puzzled by Charlie's stance but focussed on the job in hand. He was a crack shot and had won many duels in his homeland.

"Combatants are you ready?"

"Shoot!"

Charlie's right hand flew up to his pistol and as it left the holster his left hand was already sweeping across the top of the barrel to cock the hammer.

Cumberland-Smythe raised his pistol, reaching for the hammer with his thumb as it came up. His eyes widened as he saw how fast Griffon had pulled the gun from the shoulder holster and the way his left hand swept the hammer back. The last thing he saw was the barrel come into line and the flash as the charge detonated. His own gun was only halfway to the ready position.

The bullet from Charlie's gun entered just below Cumberland-Smythe's armpit, passed inside his shoulder blade and exited out the centre of his back. He was very lucky it didn't hit anything vital. It did, however, do enough damage to put him on the deck, would hurt like hell for weeks until it healed and every time the weather changed for years to come.

Charlie watched him fall and as soon as the M.C. declared him the winner, retrieved his pistol from where it had been dropped. Annabelle looked confused and glanced towards the funnel as if expecting to see someone. She visibly grimaced when Etherton stepped out from behind it and waved.

Cumberland-Smythe was taken to the ship's hospital where Dr Warburton would patch him up. Annabelle accompanied him, ignoring Charlie's open armed invitation to dally with him in his cabin.

"By gad," exclaimed Farrington, "rummest duel I've ever seen. That is a very odd technique if ever I saw one."

"A good friend of mine came up with it to get a shot of quickly, accuracy comes with practice. I have sent many rounds down a range getting it perfect."

"Well, its unconventional but worked so who am I to gainsay it. Good show by the way, didn't like that fella, something rather odd about him."

"You found our stalker where we thought he would be?"

"He was laid out with his eye to the telescopic sight. Never 'eard me coming. Gave him a rap on the bonce with my cosh."

"What happened to the gun?"

"Threw it overboard, funny calibre thing, no good for us."

"And the stalker?"

"Tied him up, gagged him and tethered him to the funnel. When he comes around, he should be able to work himself loose in a day or so."

The King George IV slipped into Bombay and the majority of the passengers disembarked. With them went Annabelle and Cumberland-Smythe who needed to rest and heal. Charlie knew this wasn't the last he would see of them. There was no sign of the stalker who they went to collect with several burly sailors and the ship's master at arms. He had disappeared, leaving just the tether and ropes behind where he had been tied up.

Charlie resisted the temptation to go ashore, India could be a dangerous place at the best of times, let alone when you had deadly enemies in the area. In any case, the packet was only going to stay in port for a single day to replenish enough stores to get them to Karachi.

There was a knock on the door to their cabin,

"Mr Griffon could you come to the dining room please there is an officer of the Bombay police here who would like to talk to you," a steward said.

In the dining room several of the first-class passengers were assembled including the colonel. A slim uniformed policeman with rank insignia, stood among them taking notes on a flip pad. He wore a bowler hat that had a pair of tinted goggles secured above the brim and there were pouches on his belt which held handcuffs, a nightstick, pistol, and, presumably, spare ammunition.

"Mr Griffon? Inspector Datta Inamdar, Bombay police," he said in an educated accent that wouldn't go amiss in Oxford.

"Pleased to meet you, how can I help?"

"We have received a complaint from a Mr Cumberland-Smythe that you maliciously wounded him. Do you have anything to say?"

"Well for one it was a perfectly legitimate duel, as my fellow passengers will probably already have testified, second I bore the man no malice or I would have killed him and third it was over the attentions of his paramour Miss Annabelle Darwimple who had initiated a liaison with me."

"Yes, that agrees with what I have been told already. However, his complaint is that you didn't comply to the rules of combat."

"How is that a matter for the police?"

"In Bombay the rules for duelling are enshrined in law."

"May I ask the captain a question?"

Inspector Inamdar nodded.

"Captain, what was the ship's position at the time of the duel?"

"I would have to look at the log for our exact position but at dawn that day we were about six-hundred miles out from Bombay on a track from Madagascar which would put us in the middle of the Arabian Sea."

"Is that in Indian national waters?"

"Not at all."

"Well you see, Inspector, as the duel was fought in International Waters the law of the nation the ship was registered in will apply, and that is Britain," Charlie said.

The inspector nodded and folded his notebook shut with a snap, "Case closed."

He stepped towards the door, "Mr Griffon, I would take great care that you do not break the law in India. There are people who would like you to be locked up and out of the way it would seem."

Charlie nodded in acknowledgement as the inspector smiled, then left.

Chapter 3: Karachi

Ten years before, Karachi had been nothing more than a fortified fishing village living life at the pace dictated by the tides. Now it was a thriving centre of commerce since The Company had taken it over and developed it beyond recognition.

The docks were busy and teeming with Indian labourers loading sacks into nets for steam cranes to either load onto ships or the truck-beds of goods trains to be shipped all over Northern India.

What caught Charlie's eye were the dirigibles that seemed to drift across the sky from all points of the compass centred on a point on the North-western edge of the city. He dawdled on the observation deck watching the activity and taking in the sight of the city at large. Suddenly something caught his eye on the dock and he sought the telescope he had hanging from his belt.

He had to search to pick up the person but when he did, "So, you are still with us my friend."

"Who?" Etherton said from behind him.

"Him." Charlie passed him the glass and pointed to the figure making his way stealthily across the port by moving from stack to stack.

"Well I never, thought he would have got off in Bombay." He handed back the glass, "Shame I could top him from here if my rifle weren't in the luggage." When he had been in the army Etherton was not only Charlie's batman but a crack shot and sniper.

"Anyway, it's time to get ashore, the luggage is on its way to the hotel and they want to turn her around." He handed Charlie his top hat which was adorned with various brass gadgets and goggles. Fashionable but useful as well.

They were booked into the Ritz, undoubtedly the best hotel in town and not anywhere near as expensive as one might think.

"We have the Presidents' Suite with connected servants' quarters," the receptionist said and rang the bell for the bellboys without waiting for Charlie to agree.

Etherton sniffed, he was happy. The servants' quarters had their own kitchen so he could prepare proper food not the stuff the Indians served up. He didn't approve of all those spices and stuff, but if he was honest, he hadn't really tried them, only seen the food served by the roadside vendors.

A troop of bellboys took their luggage and one showed them to their room. The hotel was equipped with elevators, each manned by a uniformed driver who the bellboy told which floor. A large brass lever with up and down inscribed on the backplate controlled the motion. A dead man's handle activated the drive; if the driver let it go and allowed it to spring into the off position the lift would stop dead.

Charlie watched as the driver closed the gates; the outer first, to close off the shaft, then the inner for the cabin. He held the dead man's handle in his left hand and pressed it down against the stop, then eased the drive lever towards the up position. The lift started to move, and he gradually increased the speed. Their suite was on the top floor, the sixth, and as they passed the fifth the driver eased the lever back to the neutral position until the lift stopped exactly level with the floor. He let the dead man's handle go and opened the gates.

"I must say that was skilfully done," Charlie said as he stepped out and slipped him a rupee tip. The man grinned, openly delighted to be praised.

The suite was luxurious with a massive bed. Charlie smiled; your British pound went a long way in India. He checked it for softness, then decided to leave Etherton to it and explore.

Karachi was growing and buildings were going up everywhere. The air was rich with the smell of spices, smoke from the steam shovels and cranes and human waste. It was noisy and busy. For protection, Charlie carried a silver-topped cane that had a twenty-inch blade concealed in it and his pistols. His waistcoat had fine chainmail concealed between the inner and outer layers making it stab proof.

It was late afternoon and very hot. His fashionable coat was heavy, the waistcoat chafed. He saw a shop for dirigible and train tickets and entered. It was cooler, a punkah wafted back and forth, powered from a lay shaft.

"Can I help you, sir?" an Indian clerk in a dark suit, high-collared shirt and bowtie said from behind a desk.

"Yes, I am here to do some mountain climbing on Malubiting and was wondering which was the best way to get there."

Another unprepared aristocrat concluded the clerk taking in the quality clothes and his clean-shaven face.

"The trains do not go as far as there, sir. You could go up the river by steamboat and hire horses to take you into the mountains, but you will end up walking the last twenty miles or so."

"Or?"

"You could hire a dirigible; it will cost more as the gas is imported by ship but will get you as far as the Hopar valley."

"That sounds excellent, can you arrange the hire?"

"No, sir, we only sell tickets for the regular service, you must visit the airfield and talk to one of the independent captains yourself."

Charlie left after thanking the helpful man and tipping him with a silver half guinea. He looked around for a cab but the only conveyance he could see was a strange contraption that was like a dogcart pulled by a bicycle.

"Do you take passengers?" he asked the turbaned man dressed in just a loincloth sat on the bicycle.

"Yes Sahib, very fast service, very cheap."

"Can you take me to the airfield?"

"Of course, Sahib, please climb in it will be two rupees."

Charlie calculated that was about thruppence and said, "Take me to a bank first please I need to change some money. What is your name?"

"Gupta, Sahib,"

Gupta stood on the pedals to get the thing moving and once momentum had been achieved sat, his wiry legs pumping the peddles like pistons.

"Where is the Sahib wanting to go?"

"To the airport."

"No, where does the Sahib want to go from the airport."

"To the mountains."

"I know who you need to talk to, he is the third cousin of my brother's wife and has his own craft."

Charlie was frankly sceptical and was prepared for the worst as they swung in through the gates. The airfield was not as big as he had imagined it would be and there were only four mooring poles in view. Two had dirigibles painted in company colours moored to them and must be used on regular routes. As he watched one's propellers started to turn and it backed away from the mooring.

"That is the daily service to Bombay, the other is to Jodhpur and leaves tomorrow."

The third pole was empty and had a gang of men stood ready to receive an incoming flight. They rode straight past it and headed to the furthest pole where a rather worn-looking craft was moored, passing a compound that was protected by a high fence and guards where gas cylinders were stacked.

As they approached the vessel, Charlie smiled, the envelope looked patched and weather stained, the propellers, while tarnished, looked sound and looks can be deceiving. The man who stood at the foot of the steps looked like a villain out of a penny dreadful. Short, stocky, his turban greasy, grey loose shirt and trousers that had once been white. A pair of goggles sat precariously on top of the turban and a long-hooked-knife hung from his belt.

"Gupta!" he called as they rode up, followed by a torrent of Indian. After Gupta jumped off the bicycle and clasped arms with him, he turned to Charlie, "This is Ranish, he is captain of this airship."

Charlie climbed out of the *ek saikil riksha* as he had learnt the bicycle contraption was called and made a show of looking over the dirigible. He even flipped down lenses that were hinged to the brim of his hat.

"You, Captain, are a fraud," he said and when Ranish looked angry continued, "that is a perfectly good airship made to look like a wreck. Smuggler?"

Ranish laughed showing a significant gap between his front teeth, he opened his mouth to say something when there was the sound of a distant shot and Charlie fell forward onto the ground.

Charlie gasped for breath and rolled onto his back. Ranish was yelling orders and several of his crew were racing across the field guns in hand.

"Sahib. Oh, Sahib, are you hurt?" Gupta was distraught. Ranish knelt and helped Charlie to sit up. He looked at the hole in his coat between his shoulder blades and stuck his finger inside.

"I am not the only fraud, my friend, take off your coat."

Charlie shrugged out of his coat and now Ranish could see the shine of the chain inside the torn back of the waistcoat. A lead bullet was splayed and embedded in the mesh. He worked it free and handed it to Charlie.

"You are lucky, my friend, the range it was fired from meant it didn't have enough energy to penetrate the chain."

"Tell my back that," Charlie groaned.

Ranish glared in the direction his men had run.

"You have been attacked while in my house, your enemy is now mine," he helped Charlie to his feet, "and, my friend, you are going to have one hell of a bruise."

Negotiations followed over many cups of chai and they agreed a price to hire the ship and crew by the day for as long as Charlie needed it. Charlie suspected the authorities were getting suspicious about Ranish's activities and a period out of their view was timely.

Charlie returned to the hotel and handed Etherton his coat.

"Thirty odd thirty as the Americans call it," Etherton said holding the bullet up to the light, "what range was it fired at?"

"About five hundred yards, from outside the field."

Charlie stripped of his shirt.

"That is an impressive bruise," Etherton said and moved closer to examine it.

"Haematoma, nice white centre, red ring around it turning blue and black." He gently touched the circular white central area.

"Jesus Christ! Don't do that," Charlie yelped.

"That's going to hurt for a week or so, where is the waistcoat I need to repair it."

Charlie hmphed at the lack of sympathy and pulled on a loose shirt, wincing as it brushed his back,

"I'm going to have to deal with that man permanently."

A knock at the door woke Charlie out of his slumber, he had dozed off lying on the bed on his front after Etherton had applied some liniment to his back.

Etherton opened the door and invited the person in.

"Gupta?" Charlie said as he recognised his taxi rider who was dressed in a loose vertically striped shirt and white cotton trousers.

"Yes, Sahib, it is Gupta. My cousin sends his regards and says you must wear more suitable clothes for the journey." He placed a pair of paper-wrapped bundles on the bed.

"I will get the rest."

Etherton let him out and undid the string. He held up heavy wool trousers, then, what looked like, a pair of silk under trousers.

"I think you wear these under those scratchy ones, look like your size."

Gupta returned with the more packages that contained a second set of clothes.

Dressed they looked like native mountain men. Heavy, yak wool coats belted at the waist with several layers of shirt underneath. Fur hats completed the ensemble.

"All we need are beards and we will look totally native," Charlie said.

They dressed normally to check out of the hotel at dawn the next day. Gupta organised a steam carriage to take them and their luggage to the airfield and surprised them by climbing aboard the gondola after them.

"I will come with you. I was in the company army and served in that area. I will be your guide."

Charlie had mentioned the need for a guide to Ranish and had expected him to find someone when they got to the valley. The last person he expected was Gupta.

The inside of the airship's gondola was surprisingly spacious. The steam engines were housed in an engine room at the back and were the most modern triple expansion engines available. These iron and brass beauties were a lot smaller than you would expect and generated enough power to push the airship through the air at around ten knots. Faster than a horse could maintain. The boilers were gas fired and a rack of gas bottles covered one wall.

"That's a fair investment right there," Charlie said as Ranish showed off his pride and joy.

"Customs never come in here, in fact they never enter the gondola. We keep the rotting carcass of a dog in a sealed container and when they approach; we open it by the door. The smell is awful and for some reason puts them off entering."

All the pipes that ran around the cabin and the controls were brass except the large spoked ship's wheel used for steering it. That was made of wood and was flanked by a pair of large levers.

"The wheel controls the rudder; the levers control the fins that make us go up and down."

"I have noticed something about you and Gupta, I hope you will not be offended when I say you do not look like Indians."

Ranish laughed, "That my friend is because we are Afghans."

There was a rudimentary instrument panel with a dial that showed air pressure as height. Ranish explained it was really just a barometer which they set to zero on the ground. It wasn't accurate and was useless if there was a change in the weather, but it gave them some idea of it. Another was graduated for speed and powered by a propeller mounted in a housing outside, last was a stopwatch. Beside them was something that looked like the bubble from a builder's level, mounted horizontally it showed whether they were level or banked over. Attached to the windscreen was a string that apparently showed them something called the yaw of the airship. Next to the wheel was a ship's binnacle containing a compass.

"We do not fly at night, we need to see the land so we can navigate," Ranish said.

"What about the compass? Can't you fly a heading?"

"If there is no wind, yes, but any wind will cause drift and if we cannot see the ground to estimate it, we could end up miles away from our destination."

Charlie wondered if hiring an airship was such a good idea after all.

They took off and Charlie happened to look back at the airfield as they pulled away from their mooring. A man was running towards them from the direction of the gas store waving a handful of papers. Charlie pointed him out to Gupta as Ranish was busy flying.

"He is the supervisor of the gas store, he wants the money for the gas we loaded."

Ranish grinned as he opened the valves on the engines to increase power. "I will pay him when we get back."

They rose gently to five hundred feet, according to the height indicator, and turned to head North. Ranish explained they had a wind that was blowing on their port quarter. This pushed them along, saving fuel, but also gave them some drift that had to be compensated for.

"It's a bit like sailing," Etherton said.

The others looked at him, Charlie had never sailed a boat other than as a passenger and Ranish had never been in one.

"Sailing ships give up leeway, like drift."

Ranish looked at Charlie and shrugged.

They had small sleeping cabins and as it was noticeably cooler at altitude, they decided to change into their native clothes. Back in the cabin they settled down to sorting through their climbing gear and weapons. Each rope, piton and carabiner was checked and repacked in purpose-made backpacks. These had been made to Charlie's own specification and had not only shoulder straps but a chest strap between the shoulder straps and a belt that secured them around the waist. The idea was to spread the load and not have it all on your shoulders.

Once that had been done, Charlie called Gupta to sit by him at the chart table. He took the map that Felix had provided.

"We are looking for an ancient Buddhist temple that has been lost for over a hundred years. This is a copy of an old scroll that came from a temple in China and shows that our temple is on or near Malubiting Mountain."

Gupta looked at the map, turning it this way and that. He settled it into a position that had it turned forty-five degrees from where Charlie has assumed was North up.

"This is the mountain and here you have the Hopar valley. From there, Northwest of the mountain is the Bapu Glacier. The other side of the mountain is another glacier, the Phuparash. It looks from this map that the temple is in that glacier."

"Are you sure?"

"As much as I can from this."

"How high is that glacier?"

"I do not know but it is much higher than this can fly."

"How high can we get in this?"

"I can drop us on the lower part of the Bapu Glacier, then we have to walk. I can get us some porters from Bapu village if we need them," Ranish said from the wheel.

"We?

"You will need my help, and I do not leave my friends when their enemies are nearby."

"Enemies?"

"The man who shot at you, he left town on the train heading towards Lahore."

"The train doesn't go to Lahore yet."

"That is correct, he will switch to a river boat at Moultan and at Lahore to horses. My men followed him and were waiting for a chance to kill him, but he was joined by a woman and a man. The woman was very beautiful, and the man moved like he was hurt."

Charlie exchanged a look with Etherton,

"He is, I shot him just over a week ago."

"Then next time you must make sure you kill him."

Chapter 4: Malubiting

They followed the contour of the land at five hundred feet for three days and covered over five hundred miles. Ranish flew by the seat of his pants ignoring the altimeter. He knew the land well, having run smuggled goods from Tibet and China into India for the last five years. This trip was more for fun than money, the Englishman intrigued him. He was obviously brave and had an edge of danger about him. He didn't command, he asked and said thank you. Not your typical Englishman in his experience. Added to that he had been shot while in his domain which made it a debt of honour to help him.

He looked up, the cloud cover was getting lower and the airship was steadily climbing to maintain five hundred feet above the rising ground as they rose over a line of hills. They would have to land and moor for the night earlier than he wanted.

He thought about the people who were racing them to the temple. Gupta's contacts in Karachi had told him they were Russians, that alone would be enough to put him on Charlie's side. He hated Russians. His people had been oppressed by them for years, he was a true Afghan and yearned for independence.

"Skipper, the ground is rising faster ahead." Firash's voice came through the speaking tube from his post in the lookout post at the top of the envelope. The ship had a rigid skeleton which housed the lift bags of helium. Firash was sat in an open cockpit mounted in the top of the frame.

"Prepare to land, Firash get down here and help set the mooring."

His crew of four knew the drill and would secure the ship with mooring ropes to whatever they could find. They had mooring spikes which were actually threaded iron rods that looked like augers or the part of corkscrew that went into the cork but needed at least six feet of earth to screw them into. Below them was a rocky terrain with the occasional patch of grass, stubby trees and mountain goats.

Charlie came up behind him, "Landing?"

"No choice, look."

Charlie looked up at the cloud which was lowering above them, then looked across the rocky ground and saw the goats, big animals with wicked-looking horns.

"Would one of those make good eating for supper?"

"Yes, for the next few days if you can get a big one."

Charlie went to one of the crates in their luggage and pulled out a rifle. It was an Enfield 1853 Rifle Musket. Muzzle loaded, and percussion cap fired, this rifled gun fired a Minni Ball conical bullet and was accurate to a thousand yards in the right hands.

Charlie bit the top of a cartridge, holding the ball in his mouth while he poured the powder down the barrel. He then pushed the Minni Ball into the barrel and rammed it home with the ramrod. A cap was placed on the nipple and he moved to the door which the men had opened ready to jump out and moor the ship.

There was a large one with an impressive set of horns who looked to be the dominant male and near him several females. Off to the side were a group of young males. The airship touched down and the crew piled out of the door, running for the mooring ropes. As it settled Charlie took a knee in the door and after adjusting the sight, brought the rifle to his shoulder, cocking it as he did.

Ranish watched and recognised a military-trained marksman at work. The slow breath in, the slow exhalation, the gentle squeeze of the trigger.

Dinner was a spicy billy goat and onion curry with wild rice and flat breads called Paratha. Even Etherton had to admit it was delicious. As they sat around the fire afterwards Charlie asked, "Do you think we have caught them up yet?"

"The Russians? They will be on the river to Lahore by now. We should reach the glacier ahead of them."

"You know they are Russians?"

"Yes."

Charlie decided not to ask how, he guessed it had something to do with Ranish's smuggling contacts. However, Gupta chipped in, "One of my friends took them from the railway station to their hotel. It was the one favoured by Russian traders and he helped them with their luggage. He heard the woman talk to the desk and she spoke in Russian."

"Did he say how the man was?"

"He moved slowly and had his arm in a sling. There was another man who met them there who helped him inside. He remembered him because he wore a heavy coat with a fur collar despite the heat."

Charlie grinned, leaned back to rest against the pack he was using as a backrest and pulled out a cigar.

The next morning there was a strong wind from the West which Ranish judged too much for the airship to fight. So, they had a leisurely breakfast and waited. Just before midday the wind dropped and swung more to the South. It was time to leave.

They continued to follow climbing ground for another three hours then they crested the ridge and headed down into a valley.

Ranish tapped a gauge, "We need to take on water, I will land at Jaglot and fill up."

Jaglot was on a river.

"Wouldn't want to fall in there," Etherton said, "it's ice cold and an absolute torrent."

Charlie looked down into the rapids that ran past the town at least five feet below his feet in a rocky cut.

"Comes off a glacier probably, we are in the foothills of the mountains now."

The crew had moored the airship to a tree and a large rock then fed a pipe from the gondola down into the river. A vacuum pump drew water up into the holding tank in the canopy.

"Do you think there are any fish in it?" Etherton said, a look of longing on his face.

"Did you bring a rod?"

"Just my little telescopic one."

"Then why don't you drop a line in and find out,"

Charlie knew that one of Etherton's few passions in life was the pursuit of freshwater fish. He spent his days off North of London on one of the many tributaries of the Thames, trying to persuade trout to take a fly. Charlie was happy to let him as it kept him out of trouble.

It took five minutes for Etherton to retrieve his tackle and get a line in the water. It took five minutes after that for a number of locals to gather wondering what he was doing. The crew were starting to haul up the pipe, the tank being full, when he got a bite. His four-foot rod bent as something grabbed his bait and was impaled by the hook.

"Woohoo! Got one!"

He made his way down the bank totally focussed on the fight followed by a crowd of locals that was growing by the second.

"Ready when you are," Ranish said from the doorway, then noticed the excited mob.

"Going to have to wait until Etherton either pulls that fish out or it drowns him."

"Does he do this often?"

"Every chance he gets."

It took him half an hour to bring the fish to shore and he returned to the airship smiling happily, the fish held up for all to see. It was similar to a brown trout in shape, greeny-brown on the upper body with a light brown stripe about an inch wide down its side. Charlie guessed it was probably three to four pounds.

"Do you see it! Isn't it magnificent!" Etherton said, a beaming smile on his face.

"Yes, it's lovely. Now get in the airship we have to get moving."

Etherton cast one last long, longing look at the foaming water, imagining what other prizes were hidden in its depths, then made his way after Charlie into the ship.

"I will come back here one day with my best rods, the locals said that there were even bigger fish than this one in that river," Etherton said as he served Charlie a fried fillet of the fish for dinner that evening.

"It's certainly tasty, not muddy like the trout in England."

"That's the water."

"Really?"

Etherton saw he was beginning to bore Charlie with his fish talk so changed the subject. "How far now?"

"Ranish says we have to swing around to the Northwest of the mountain to land on the Bapu Glacier. We should be there tomorrow evening."

They landed on the glacier at just before dark and the crew worked hard to drive spikes into the ice to secure the airship. The wind was picking up and icy flakes of snow were scudding across the surface stinging their faces. The temperature was well below freezing and wind chill dropped it even further.

Ranish kept the boiler for the engines running to keep pumping hot water through the water tanks to stop them freezing. Small auxiliary burners provided just enough warmth to keep the cabins above freezing. They slept in their clothes and in the morning, as the sun rose, they breakfasted on porridge laced with honey.

Charlie, Gupta and Etherton shrugged into their backpacks, they were well wrapped up and wore boots with hobnails in the soles to provide grip. Charlie had his rifle in a holster fixed to the right side of his pack where he could reach it easily. Ranish and Firash appeared similarly dressed, carrying packs and armed,

"We will be coming with you, there are at least three Russians and I expect they will have hired help."

Charlie smiled behind the leather mask and goggles he wore to protect his face. He stepped out behind Gupta who led, using ski poles to help keep his balance and headed towards the mountain that dominated the skyline to the Southeast. The sun was soon glaring off the ice and snow and they all flipped smoked glass lenses down over their goggles to protect against snow blindness. The going was hard, they were climbing steadily and even the hobnails barley stopped them slipping.

Gupta called a halt, produced a coil of rope and tied them all together with about fifteen feet of rope between each of them. The visibility had reduced to no more than that and he navigated by following the slope as much as anything else. Eventually the snow stopped, and he led them onto a rocky trail that followed a contour line around the mountain. They entered a slot in the rocks that was like a passageway. The walls coated in ice. They were sheltered from the constant wind and the silence was profound.

Etherton shifted the rope so the knot wasn't digging into his side. "Do we still need to be tethered?"

Gupta stopped and pointed ahead.

The path they were following exited from the passage and followed a cliff face as a ledge no more than a foot wide. Etherton looked down and gulped. It was two hundred feet straight down to the floor of a canyon.

They edged along testing each step before they put weight on it. The rock was frost cracked and large flakes would sheer off and tumble down into the canyon without notice. The ledge got even narrower and they had to edge along with their backs to the icy rock wall. They started to get cold, it seeped into their bones from the contact with the rock and as soon as they reached ground wide enough to take a rest they stopped.

Charlie slipped his arms out of his pack and swung it around in front of him. He dug inside and produced a small alcohol stove and a collapsible pot. This ingenious device folded almost flat when packed and extended up to make a pot some five inches deep when needed. He filled the pot with fresh snow and put it on the stove which he lit with one of the Vesuvian outdoor matches he carried in a metal box. Etherton dug into his pack and produced a small folding screen that acted as a windbreak for the stove and an oiled paper packet of tealeaves. Soon they were all sipping mugs of hot black tea and eating chunks of Kendal mint cake. Suitably refreshed and energised they set off again, determined to cover as much ground as possible before dark.

The next morning, they packed away their tents and set off again. Gupta assured them they would reach the head of the Phuparash glacier by the end of the day. Charlie was impatient, the Russians couldn't be that far behind them, but tempted as he was to rush forward, he knew that that was a quick route to disaster. They advanced with caution.

Gupta made his way forwards onto an ice bridge over a chasm close to the glacier. It looked solid enough and he edged forward until he was almost to the middle. He reached forward and tested the ice ahead of him with one of his sticks. There was a crack that sounded as loud as a rifle shot and the bridge ahead of him crazed as cracks spread out from the iron tip. He froze, stooped over not daring to move. When nothing happened, he slowly stood and turned to face the rest of the team. He raised his hands as if to say, 'that was close' and disappeared with a look of absolute surprise as he dropped straight down as the bridge collapsed.

Charlie was next in line and instinctively braced himself as Gupta's weight came on the line, but he was dragged forward, feet slipping towards the gaping maw. Etherton had time to jam his boot against a rock and as the rope between him and Charlie tightened, held his position. Ranish and Firash likewise managed to brace and the three of them halted the advance towards the edge and helped pull a terrified Gupta back onto the path.

Charlie helped Gupta sit on a pack. "Are you alright?"

Gupta said nothing just stared into space. Ranish came and sat next to him talking in his native tongue. Charlie stood at the edge of the chasm and looked at the path that continued on the other side for another thirty yards before reaching the glacier.

"I think if we get a grapnel across and lodged between those two rocks we could get the lightest of us over to secure another rope for the rest of us to cross."

Etherton stood beside him and eyed the gap. "I think I can hit that."

He pulled his rifle from its holster on his pack and unclipped a folded grapnel from the array of climbing aids dangling from the steel ring on the other side. The grapnel tines, when folded, formed the streamlined shape of a pinecone and a long shaft protruded below them. Just below the tines was a steel ring and Etherton set about splicing a rope to it. Happy that it was properly secure he loaded his gun with a blank charge that had a thick leather wad tamped down on top of it, then slid the shaft into the barrel. He lifted the gun to his shoulder, noting it was now horribly nose heavy.

"Sahib stop!" Gupta suddenly cried.

Etherton lowered the gun and turned to look as the animated man came up to them.

"Look," Gupta stood at the edge and pointed down into the chasm, "I saw that when I was hanging from the rope."

Charlie looked. At first he couldn't see anything but then he picked out the darker shape against the dark rock.

"What is it?"

"A cave or tunnel."

Charlie pulled off his gloves and took out the map.

"It says here, 'pass through the dark and into the light to receive Buddha's blessing,' I thought that was just a religious slogan."

"Maybe it refers to a tunnel."

Etherton nodded. "We need to have a look, we could try the harpoon."

Charlie nodded and Etherton pulled the grapnel from the barrel of his gun and cut the rope from it. He selected another tool from the selection on his pack. This one had a head that looked vaguely like a harpoon but had four backward-facing tines behind the bullet-shaped head. He spliced on the rope and set it in the barrel of his rifle.

Charlie was examining the rock face opposite them with a small telescope. "There is a crack that looks about the right size just above the top of the hole. Can you see it?"

Etherton laid face down on the path on his bedroll and wrapped the shoulder strap of the rifle around his left arm. He used Charlie's pack as a rest and sighted. There was no wind but the rope would drag on the harpoon to slow it so it would drop as well. This would not be an easy shot.

He found the crack, he had exceptional long-distance vision, aimed high and to the left as the rope would drag to the right. A glance showed the rope was perfectly coiled and he sighted again. He drew in a deep breath and slowly let it out. The rifle was an American Spencer and had a hair trigger that took just a pound and a half of pressure to send the harpoon on its way.

Time slowed as he followed its path through the air and for a split-second, he thought he had missed, but the tip of the harpoon passed inside the right-hand edge of the crack. The head rammed in far enough for the tines to get a grip. A cheer went up from the entire team.

Charlie took the rope and passed it around a large rock then got Firash to help him pull it as tight as they could. After tying it off he looked along the line which sloped down at about thirty degrees and sagged slightly towards the end.

"I will go first."

He undid his safety rope and replaced it with a longer rope which he passed to Rafish.

"Let it run, I will need momentum and when I'm inside will try and find somewhere to secure it."

He sat on the edge of the chasm and looped a leather strap over the rope in front of him. He wrapped the end around his hands and took a deep breath. *Here goes nothing!*

He dropped into space and felt the jolt in his shoulders as the strap took his weight. He slid down, accelerating as gravity did its work. It took just a few seconds to be halfway down and the rock face was approaching rapidly. The rope was sagging now under his weight as it stretched, timing would be everything.

As the sag started to slow him and he was five feet from the wall he let go. He dropped and his momentum carried him feet first into the opening. The floor rushed up at him and he landed flat on his back, knocking the air out of him.

"Ouch!" he gasped as the air was knocked out of him, it was a long moment before he managed to breathe in. He pushed himself to his feet and pulled his belt around so he could reach the hammer and pitons he had hung from it. It had slipped around during his slide and he thanked the lord that he hadn't landed on it. Examining the wall, he selected a couple of cracks and hammered in pitons; the sound echoing down the passageway. Satisfied they were secure he looped his rope through the attached carabiners and made it secure.

The rest of the team sent down the packs then came down the rope one at a time. By the time Rafish arrived last they had oil lamps lit and the packs piled up along one side.

"We will leave the packs here. If the map is correct the temple is the other end of this tunnel."

"Not a cave?" Gupta asked.

"No, only the opening and the first ten feet is natural. From there on its manmade."

They moved into the dark passage that sloped gently down, the light from the oil lamps projected forward by their silvered reflectors. They came to a flight of steps and carefully, as they were slick with ice, started down. At the bottom they came to a blank wall of rock.

"A dead end? That's not right."

Charlie tapped it with his hammer, it sounded solid not hollow. He took his lamp and shone it over the face of the rock. He was about to give up when something caught his eye.

"Give me a boost." Etherton put his back to the wall and cupped his hands so Charlie could stand in them. He was thankful for his gloves as the hobnails dug in.

Charlie ran his fingers over the marks that had caught his attention. It was a stylised flame with smoke rising from the top of it. *What does that mean?* Stepping to the ground he looked around at the expectant faces. He leaned back against the wall and winced, he was bruised and wished he could have a steam bath to ease his aches. A vision of steam rising from hot rocks filled his mind.

"Smoke! We need to make some smoke!" he went back to the packs, "I need tea, sugar and rice!" Etherton and Firash produced some of each.

"Bring your stove and the pot."

Back at the wall he got Etherton to get the stove going and poured a mixture of rice, sugar, dried herbs and tea into the pot which he put on the flame.

"You will ruin it!" Etherton complained.

"I'll buy you a new one. Now watch."

The mixture took a while but then began to smoke. It rose in the cold air and Charlie tracked it with his lamp. Instead of flattening out on the ceiling of the passage it disappeared.

"I need to get up there."

Charlie took off his boots and after tying the laces together slung them around his neck. Rafish and Firash stood facing the wall, shoulder to shoulder their hands bracing them on the stone. Etherton gave Charlie a boost with his cupped hands and he stepped onto their bowed backs and then onto their shoulders.

"Together now, lift me up."

The men straightened and Charlie reached above him feeling along the rock.

"A little higher."

There was muttering from below then he rose another two feet and his hands found a cavity.

"Another six inches!" More grunting and he lifted enough to get his forearms over the edge.

"Sorry!" he said and shoved off hard with his legs as he pulled himself up and into the…passageway.

It was like the original one. Faint tool marks showed it was manmade and he could see the smoke being drawn down it. He put on his boots then lowered a rope, hauled the others up and led them forward. A faint blue light could be seen at the end of the tunnel.

They emerged into what must have once been a cave but had been enlarged massively. The far end was a wall of ice and showed evidence that it had once continued on before the glacier had ground it away.

The inside had been simply but skilfully carved in keeping with the teachings of Buddha. The dominating feature was a massive statue of the man himself, smiling benevolently down on them. He was depicted sitting in the lotus position one hand raised in blessing the other in his lap.

Charlie pulled out the map and examined all the written comments, all it said was Buddha's fist was near the statue.

"Look for hidden compartments or places something could be hidden."

He searched the plinth the statue sat on, tapping with a piton for hollows. Nothing. Etherton searched around the sides and tried to get around the back.

Where would he put a worthless lump of coal if he were Buddha? Then he had a thought.

"Gupta, how do Buddhists express contempt?"

"They stamp on the object or hit it with a shoe."

"Do they now."

Charlie climbed up onto the statue and looked closely at the hand that rested in the lap. It looked solid so he turned his attention to the feet. At first glance they looked solid then he compared them.

"Well I'm damned, Buddha has a bunion." He muttered as he noticed the left foot had a lump on it. He tapped with his piton and the surface cracked, it was plaster made to look like stone.

A couple of hard raps and the plaster fell away. A lump of rock broke off and landed on the stone with a bright clink. Charlie grinned and picked it up. It was cold and hard.

"Got it!" he called as he jumped down.

Chapter 5: Risk

The glacier groaned and the ice wall shifted about three feet tearing rocks from the cave opening, mission accomplished they retraced their steps to the mouth of the tunnel. Getting up the rope would be harder than coming down and one of them would have to go up first. Charlie volunteered.

"No, Sahib, this is a task for me," Gupta said, stepping in front of him. He didn't say it, but he saw the collapse of the bridge as his fault even if it had revealed the entrance. Not only that, he wanted to prove to himself he hadn't lost his nerve.

"If you are sure."

"Yes, Sahib."

Gupta pulled himself up on the rope using his legs and arms. He started steadily pulling himself up the thirty-degree slope. He knew it would only get harder and getting over the edge at the top would be difficult.

Two thirds of the way up the slope increased as he got past the sag in the rope and he found himself climbing in a more traditional way; pushing with his legs and pulling with his arms. He got to the top and squirmed over the edge skinning his fingers on the rock as he did.

With a man on the other side Charlie, the next one to cross, had an easier time of it as Gupta helped. The packs were slung across next and soon all of them were across. Charlie cut the ropes and let them fall, no sense in making it easy for someone else.

They made their way back to the Bapu Glacier and as soon as the airship came into view Charlie knew they had a problem. He studied the scene through his telescope as he lay behind a snow ridge. A large vehicle was standing beside it, smoke coming from a tall stack at the back of it. Instead of running directly on wheels it had a kind of belt arrangement with wheels inside it. Charlie guessed it laid its own road as it moved, constantly picking it up and laying it down. It was painted grey and had the Russian Eagle painted on the side.

What was more worrying were the uniformed men wandering around the airship.

Ranish, who was next to him, sighed. "Cossacks."

"You know them?"

"I've had to run from them a time or two. Vicious thugs in the main part."

"Looks like they have taken your men prisoner, and there are our old friends." Smythe and Annabelle climbed down from the gondola followed by the stalker.

It was a bad situation, their means of transport was in enemy hands and worse, the crew were hostages.

"What we need is a plan," Charlie said as he watched the camp. The only problem was: he didn't have one.

A ragged figure staggered down the glacier towards the airship and accompanying steam carriage. He stumbled and fell, picked himself up and staggered forward again. He was spotted by the grey uniformed soldiers and an alarm was given. Two were dispatched to bring him into the camp.

Annabelle shielded her eyes with her hand and squinted against the glare, "It's Griffon."

Charlie was half dragged half carried into the camp and thrown into the cabin of the carriage.

"Hello, Charlie." Annabelle stood over him as he fought to focus his eyes in the dim light.

"Annabelle? Is that you?"

She grabbed his chin and moved his head from side to side looking at his eyes.

"Snow blind. What happened? Where are the rest of your party?"

"Etherton, dead, the glacier," his eyes widened in horror, "the glacier took them all! It ground them to pulp!"

"Where?"

"In the temple. Gone, it's all gone!"

"Give him some vodka."

A soldier pulled a bottle from his coat pocket and pulled the cork with his teeth. He tipped Charlie's head back and poured a good slug down his throat. Charlie swallowed and coughed as the fiery liquid burnt down his gullet.

"Now tell me, what happened?"

"We found what remained of the temple, the glacier had been grinding it away for years. The statue and about five feet of rock were all that were left." Charlie slumped as if the effort was too much. The soldier bent over and poured more vodka into his mouth. Charlie coughed and spat the spirit into the man's eyes. As he reared back Charlie kicked out and his heavy boot connected with the side of the man's head. Simultaneously he grabbed Annabelle by the coat collar and pulled her towards him.

He head butted her on the forehead and she slumped unconscious to the floor. He moved quickly to the side of the door just as another soldier stuck his head through to see what was going on. The butt of the unconscious soldier's rifle put this one's lights out. Charlie dragged him inside, shut and barred the door.

A coil of rope provided him with the means to secure all three after which he pulled up his shirt and unwrapped a length of material from around his middle. The soldiers hadn't searched him thoroughly and missed the two revolvers strapped to the small of his back.

He checked that the percussion caps were still in place and moved into the control cabin. It was empty and he sat in the driver's chair to check over the controls. Two levers stood up from the floor and were locked in the rearmost position a third shorter lever was in the central position of a gated slot which was marked with arrows pointing forward and back. A rudimentary instrument panel had a pressure gauge, which showed they had a full head of steam, and a compass. There was a large valve wheel on the side.

A face appeared at the window, looked surprised and shouted something in Russian. *Now or never, old man,* he thought and spun the wheel on the valve, and pushed the two long levers forward.

He didn't know what to expect but nothing happened. There was a banging on the door as someone tried to get in. He looked around frantically and spotted that the smaller lever was vibrating in the central gate. He wrenched it into the forward position. There was a grating of gears and a lurch, then the carriage started to move. It jerked and shuddered almost throwing him out of his seat. He accidently pulled the right lever back and the world outside swung around as the carriage turned.

He saw one of the Cossacks stood about ten yards slight to the left aiming a rifle at him. He was about to duck when the soldier folded to the floor blood pooling around his head. The camp swung into view and he steered the clanking waggon to go between the airship and the captives who were clustered around the fire.

There was a thump on the roof and a blast of cold air followed by the sound of feet hitting the deck. Charlie left the seat and took up his pistols to face the door. The carriage tilted forward as it dropped into a trough and threw Charlie back against the instrument panel just as the door burst open and the stalker flew through it a long-bladed dagger in his hand.

Luckily the lurch had thrown him off balance as well and the two ended up in a tangled heap on the floor struggling, biting and gouging. Charlie had dropped his guns to fend off the knife and was in a life-or-death struggle with the wild-eyed Russian who was intent on gutting him. Meanwhile, the carriage carried on straight through the camp and toward the edge of the glacier.

The stalker managed to get on top of Charlie and was forcing the knife down towards his throat. Charlie was fending him off with his right hand, but the knife was getting closer and closer as the Russian brought more weight to bear. Charlie groped out with his left hand searching for anything he could use as a weapon. The knife was pricking his throat and a small rivulet of blood ran around his neck.

There was a muffled bang and his assailant stiffened, a double click, a second bang and he slumped down on top of Charlie. The dead weight of the man was hard to move, and Charlie had to wiggle out from beneath him. He shoved his smoking pistol into his waistband, retrieved his second pistol then looked out of the windscreen.

"OH SHIT!" He threw himself in the seat, dropped his guns in his lap and tried to pull the levers back. Only the left one moved; the man's body was jamming the right hand one in the forward position. He hauled the left one all the way back and the carriage lurched into a left turn around the stationary left drive belt. The edge of the glacier slid by right under his nose, the right belt running half on and half off the edge. As soon as he could see the camp again Charlies forced the drive lever into the central position. The carriage stopped.

Charlie slumped in the chair and breathed a sigh of relief. Then an arm wrapped around his neck. He grabbed a pistol and cocked it, pointed it over his shoulder and pulled the trigger. The arm let go and he looked down to see the stalker staring back at him from a single eye. The other having been destroyed by the bullet passing through it into his brain.

He went into the cabin; Annabelle was awake and looking in horror at the dead man in the driver's cabin.

The rest of the camp was a running fight. The Cossacks fought the Afghans and Charlie walked through it firing his pistols, killing soldiers as he went. It was soon over.

Etherton walked over, his rifle over his shoulder.

"That was fun! Thought you were going over the edge there for a minute."

"Yes, close call that. Where is Smythe?"

"Here," Etherton's eyes widened and Charlie turned slowly around. Cumberland-Smythe stood, pistol in hand, right behind him. Charlie could see right down the barrel.

"Where is Ivan?"

"Is that his name? In the carriage; dead a bullet through the brain."

"Anna will be most upset; he is her brother."

"Oh, she knows already and you're right she wasn't happy."

"I will hold you down while she cuts out your heart."

"I don't think so, at least not today."

Cumberland-Smythe was about to ask why, when his eyes rolled up in his head and he slumped to the ground. Gupta appeared from behind him as he fell, a pistol held by the barrel in his hand.

Chapter 6: Not Entirely a Pleasure Cruise

They returned to Karachi. Cumberland-Smythe and Annabelle were left tied up in their steam carriage with the boiler running so they didn't freeze. The local villagers were told they were there, and Charlie paid the headman to send someone to let them go after they had left.

"You know that we will be bound to see them again, you made an enemy out of her when you killed her brother."

"He didn't give me a lot of choice and anyway they started it."

Etherton shrugged and held his peace. Charlie had a sense of fair play he learnt on the playing fields of Charterhouse. He was quite incapable of cold-blooded murder while not batting an eyelid when dispatching an enemy in a fight.

He grabbed a handhold as the airship lurched. It was battling against the wind which had aided them on the journey to the mountains.

"Sahib, Charlie, I think it is best you get off at Kundian and take the river steamer until you can get a train to Karachi. With this wind it will take me weeks," Ranish said.

Charlie didn't take a lot of persuading; they were flying at the time of year when sane airship captains put their craft in hangars for their annual maintenance.

Kundian was a typical Northern Indian town. Cows wandered around freely, their faces decorated with paint and horns festooned with flower garlands. It was getting cold as winter was setting in and the men were wrapped in yak's wool coats. Charlie and Etherton fit right in dressed in their native clothes. Gupta shepherded them through the town.

The railway station was a stark contrast to the rest of the town, which, to be frank, was scruffy. The manager obviously took pride in his position and his charge. It was like stepping into a British country garden. The stone flags of the platform and ticket hall were continuously swept clean by a pair of young boys who worked their way back and forth endlessly. Pots of flowers and window boxes decorated the platform and the woodwork was freshly painted and spotless.

"You are in luck, sir, the train to Karachi will be here tomorrow around midday," the ticket clerk told him, "would you like two first-class tickets?" The man obviously thought Gupta didn't qualify for one. When Charlie asked for three Gupta just touched his arm and shook his head. So Charlie said, "Yes please. Is there a hotel we can stay in tonight?"

"I can recommend the one across the road from the station entrance."

"Who runs it?" Gupta said.

"My uncle, the brother of the manager."

"A family business," Charlie said as they dumped their bags in the neat and surprisingly well-appointed rooms.

"Not unusual, Sahib, family is very important."

Gupta had argued he would find his own accommodation, but Charlie would have none of it and the three of them would share the suite.

The rooms had a bathroom that was fed from the central boiler which was old, wood fired and delivered water through banging and clanking pipes. Charlie filled the bath and slid gratefully into its warm embrace.

Gupta, meanwhile, went out to source their evening meal and returned as Charlie was finishing getting dressed. He was accompanied by a pair of boys, each carrying what looked like a stack of cake tins held together in an ingenious frame with a handle attached to the top.

Inside each tin was a different component of their meal: thin and crispy naan breads, saffron-scented rice, spicy mutton sheekh kebabs with a yoghurt and mint sauce, a mutton curry that was hot with pepper and chilli, some roasted chicken that had been marinated in a mix of yoghurt, chilli, coriander and mint and roasted in a tandoor, a mixed vegetable curry, a sweet mango pickle and a fiery lime chutney. If that wasn't enough there was a desert of delicate whey dough balls steeped in sugar syrup called Gulab Jamun and a bright red spiral of fried batter called Jilapi also soaked in syrup flavoured with lime juice.

Gupta tried to get them to eat Indian style by using bread to scoop up the meat, veg and rice but the Englishmen produced cunningly-designed cutlery that clipped together in the minimum of space for travelling. Appetites sated, all three sat and talked until Charlie declared it was time for bed.

The following morning, they crossed the road to the station. Porters from the hotel carried their dunnage and deposited it on the platform. It was eleven o'clock.

Two hours later, Charlie bought three cups of cardamom-scented, sweet tea from a chi wallah who served hot chi with much ceremony and drama pouring the tea from one glass into another to aerate it. There was no sign of the train and no information as to when it would arrive.

Two more cups of chi and there was a hint of steam approaching down the track. That resolved into the unmistakeable black shape of a large, broad gauge engine with smoke billowing from its tall chimney stack and steam hissing from its sides. As usual in the sub-continent people clung to the sides and sat on the roof of the second- and third-class carriages. As soon as it stopped, with the first-class carriage precisely in front of where they stood, porters grabbed their bags and carried them on, leaving them to follow.

Gupta had steadfastly refused to travel in first class and insisted they buy him a second-class ticket. Nothing Charlie or Etherton said had moved him. When they got onboard Charlie understood why. First class was filled exclusively with Europeans and high-class Indians dressed in rich clothes and jewels. The staff were in railway livery and had a haughtiness that shouted louder than anything that they were superior to all other workers on the railroad.

"Good job we dressed in our regular clothes," Etherton said.

It took two days to reach Karachi where Gupta found them transport from the station to the Savoy.

"The Packet isn't due for another two weeks," Etherton said after he had made enquiries at the ticket office, "and not a single company ship in port."

"That's no good. The Russians will have caught up with us by then!"

"I know, which is why I have us booked on a steamer leaving tomorrow that will get us to Bombay. We should be able to find a company ship leaving from there for England."

The steamer was nothing more than a large coaster, owned and run by the East India Company. It had an Indian captain and crew and was carrying a cargo of rice. It was passed its prime and they were given a small cabin with bunk beds as it would be a two-day run.

Just after dawn on the second day, the lookout called that there was an airship coming up behind them. Charlie made his way up to the bridge and looked at it through his telescope. It looked military, even though he could see no national insignia.

"That's a scout ship, normally used by the Army," Etherton said, peering through a large telescope he had borrowed from the captain. "It's armed as well; I can see a rack of bombs below the gondola." He handed Charlie the glass.

As the airship caught them up, he could make out the faces of people in the gondola. One of them was familiar.

"We had better get our guns, if I'm not mistaken that is Annabelle and where she is, Smythe isn't far away."

He turned to the captain, "How close are we to the Bombay protection zone?" He was referring to the area patrolled by the company's airships.

"At least half a day."

"If you have weapons onboard, I suggest you issue them."

Charlie had his Enfield and Etherton his Spencer as they waited for the airship to come into range. They had created a bulwark of rice sacks and were supported by a couple of the crew with ancient muskets.

"I wonder how they managed to catch us up?" Charlie said as he adjusted his sights to maximum range. The wind was on their stern and light.

The captain shrugged, Charlie had filled him in on who was chasing them without telling him about the diamond.

There was a puff of smoke from the door of the airship which had yawed to one side to allow someone to take a shot. A moment later a bullet whined off the metal roof of the bridge.

"Our turn!"

Charlie settled and took careful aim. The range was just under one-thousand yards.

"You missed!" the captain said.

"No, he didn't," Etherton said and squeezed off his shot.

Both men quickly reloaded, taking their time to make sure the bullets were seated properly.

A bullet smacked into the sack in front of Charlie.

"Someone up there doesn't like you."

"The feeling is mutual."

Charlie fired again, followed by Etherton whose bullet hit the bomb rack.

"Nice shot!"

"Thank you."

One of the crew fired but the airship was beyond the range of his musket.

"Save it until you can see the whites of their eyes," Etherton barked, then ducked as the enemy sniper sent a shower of rice grains over him with his next shot.

"I think they mean to bomb us," Charlie said. "Captain, be ready to put on full right rudder when I tell you."

The airship was running up to them at around five hundred feet and a man was leaning out of the door. Charlie took aim then changing his mind shifted to another target.

His gun barked and he yelled, "NOW!"

The bullet passed through the thin metal of the gondola right in front of where the pilot should be stood, and the airship swung away just as they released a bomb. That and the ship veering as the captain put on full rudder was enough to ruin their aim and it exploded twenty yards off their port quarter. Etherton fired and the man in the door jerked before falling into the sea.

Charlie abandoned precision loading for speed and tap loaded his next round. This time he aimed for the rear part of the gondola that housed the engine and was rewarded by the sound of a load clang as he hit something inside. Now the airship was close enough for the crew to join in as it swung back towards them to run in for a beam attack.

Charlie shot for the pilot again.

"Zig-zag!" he called to the captain.

Etherton shot at the bomb rack again and again the sound of his bullet ricocheting off the bombs or the frame showed he was on target.

A hail of bullets from the gondola door sent them under cover and the airship passed directly over them. They braced, expecting a bomb to fall. Nothing happened and they all jumped up and fired again.

Charlie's bullet entered the rear of the envelope and he saw it exit through the front. Etherton went for the engine compartment.

The airship turned to make another run and they frantically reloaded. Charlie could see them open the door on the other side to the one they had been shooting from and a gun poke out. He was just taking aim on the point he thought the shooter would be when a cloud of steam erupted from the door and the propellers slowed and stopped. At the mercy of the wind the airship slowed then started to drift.

"Captain! Full speed for Bombay!" Charlie shouted. "Good shot, Etherton, you must have damaged their boiler."

"Or cut a pipe. Are they losing height?"

Charlie studied the crippled airship. "I believe they are. Let's put a couple more through their envelope."

They carried on shooting at the airship's envelope until they were out of range.

Bombay was a welcome sight as were the half dozen company ships in the harbour. The last they had seen of the airship it was sinking very slowly towards the sea. Charlie wondered if they got the engine running again and the holes in the gas bags closed enough to get them to land.

Once on shore, they enquired as to which was the first ship to England and were told that two were leaving first thing the next morning. Both were big, typical, East Indiamen. They visited the company's shipping office and learnt that the Hindustan had room for two more club passengers to Cape Town where a first-class cabin would become available.

Club cabins at least had a porthole and were for better off second-class passengers. Not what Charlie was used to, but they needed to get on their way as soon as possible so he paid up and shut up.

As he was leaving the office he almost bumped into a rather beautiful, very well-dressed woman.

"I'm so sorry," he said as he grabbed her arm to steady her.

"You should – oh hello," she said as she looked into his eyes.

Hazel eyes that were flecked with green met his. Charlie stepped back and bowed, clearing the way for her to enter the office. As she entered through the door, she cast a look back over her shoulder her coiffured blond hair tumbling over her shoulder.

The Hindustan left on time giving Charlie just enough time to send a telegraph message to Felix telling of their success, he would meet them on their arrival. Charlie decided that he would have to spend the days of the first leg of the trip on the leisure deck as the cabin was just too cramped. He found himself a deck chair and settled down to read.

He was halfway through the second chapter of the rather melancholic romance he had picked up in Bombay when he was aware that someone was stood casting a shadow across him. His hand moved towards his revolver as he looked up.

He relaxed. The woman from the office stood looking down at him from beneath a parasol.

"Hello," she said.

"Hello."

"I didn't see you at lunch in the dining room."

"That's because I could only get a club cabin for my man and I until the Cape."

She sat in the chair next to him and a teasing look twinkled in her eyes.

"You must have been desperate to leave India, were you being pursued by an enraged husband?"

Charlie laughed. "Not as such, but there was an enraged woman involved."

"Really, that sounds absolutely fascinating you must tell me more."

The trip home suddenly looked like it would be much more enjoyable.

Author's Note

This novella was an experiment to see if I could write outside of the fairly rigid constraints of a true historical novel. I have always enjoyed the idea of steampunk, an alternative history where steam is the predominant energy source, and mechanical engineering is pushed to different limits.

The Charlamagne Griffon Chronicles will be a series of standalone novels about Charlie and Etherton's adventures. I hope you enjoyed this brief introduction to them.